# NEVER UNDERESTIMATE
# YOUR DUMBNESS

DON'T DUMBLY READ MY DIARY!!!

## Think you can handle another Jamie Kelly diary?

# DEAR DUMB DIARY,

## NEVER UNDERESTIMATE YOUR DUMBNESS

BY JAMIE KELLY

## SCHOLASTIC INC.

New York   Toronto   London   Auckland   Sydney
Mexico City   New Delhi   Hong Kong   Buenos Aires

*For Craig Walker, without whom there might never have been a Dear Dumb Diary.*

ISBN-13: 978-0-439-82596-2

ISBN-10: 0-439-82596-2

17 16                                                    13/0

Printed in the U.S.A.                                    40

First printing, March 2008

# This Diary
# Property of:

*Jamie Kelly*

SCHOOL: Mackerel Middle School

Best friend: Isabella

Expert on: CUTENESS, DUMBNESS

Least favorite color: Gross-colored

Least favorite thing about CLOTHING: POOFYNESS

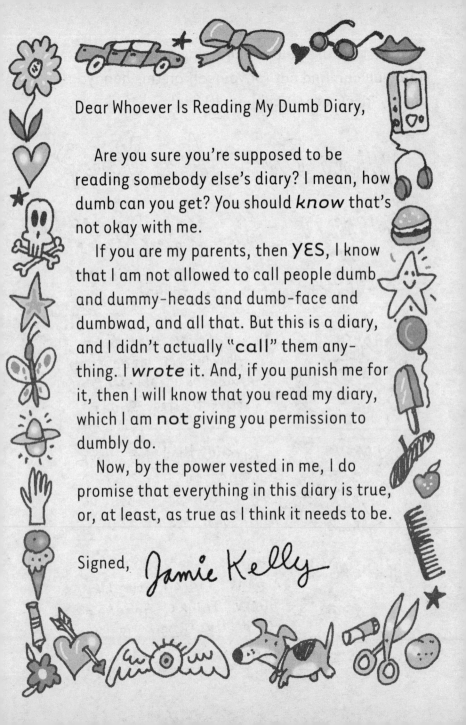

Dear Whoever Is Reading My Dumb Diary,

Are you sure you're supposed to be reading somebody else's diary? I mean, how dumb can you get? You should *know* that's not okay with me.

If you are my parents, then YES, I know that I am not allowed to call people dumb and dummy-heads and dumb-face and dumbwad, and all that. But this is a diary, and I didn't actually "call" them anything. I *wrote* it. And, if you punish me for it, then I will know that you read my diary, which I am **not** giving you permission to dumbly do.

Now, by the power vested in me, I do promise that everything in this diary is true, or, at least, as true as I think it needs to be.

Signed, Jamie Kelly

**PS:** Just in case you're wondering how dumb you are, you can find out for yourself on this handy, highly-accurate, Dumbness IQ Scale:

# How Dumb Are You?

 **NINNY** EATS stuff that has fallen on floor. Loses things often. Likes sound of busy signal.

 **BUFFOON** Believes that Baby Powder is made from powdered Babies. PANTS frequently too SHORT.

 **DUMMY** Afraid that her toys come to life at night. Likes taste of her own SNEEZES.

 **IDIOT** Thinks that recycling means riding your bike AGAIN. Thinks Angeline is pretty. BRAIN is SOLID Brick of fudge.

# Sunday 01

Dear Dumb Diary,

How would you feel if your uncle ate your sock and pooped on your lawn?
- a)    I'd feel grossed out.
- b)    I'd feel so grossed out, I could never be grossed in again.
- c)    I'd feel like staying on the porch.

I would choose all three. My uncle didn't do it, but my dog has, and for some reason, we just go out there and clean it up without calling the police — which we **will** do if an uncle ever does it. (Hey, uncles! I'm not kidding. Take the hint if you're reading this.)

Uncle in JAiL foR
GROSSNESS in the FiRST DEGREE

Will I ever understand why we put up with a dog whose main purpose in life is to perform odors and get tripped over? How dumb are we?

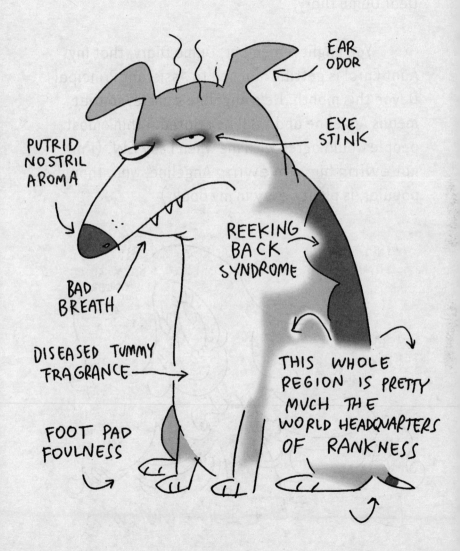

EAR ODOR

EYE STINK

PUTRID NOSTRIL AROMA

REEKING BACK SYNDROME

BAD BREATH

DISEASED TUMMY FRAGRANCE

THIS WHOLE REGION IS PRETTY MUCH THE WORLD HEADQUARTERS OF RANKNESS

FOOT PAD FOULNESS

# Monday 02

Dear Dumb Diary,

   You might remember, Dumb Diary, that my Aunt Carol is getting married to Assistant Principal Devon this month. He's Angeline's uncle, so that means Angeline and I will be related. I think most people would agree with me when I say **EW**. (I'm not **ewing** him, I'm **ewing** Angeline, who, though popular, is plenty **ewy** in my book.)

NASTY BLONDE SHIMMERING

EYES A HIDEOUS BABY BLUE COLOR

CHEEKS HAVE TERRIBLE PINKISH HUE

UNPLEASANTLY PLEASANT SMILE

EEEEEEEWWWW

Since he is my assistant principal, and not a person, it's difficult to think of him as my Uncle Dan. I'm thinking of calling him something like "Uncle Assistant Principal Devon."

He used to be really nice, but he seems frowny nowadays and kind of moody.

Isabella says it's because he's getting married and that people sometimes get a little moody as the Big Day approaches because they're practicing for married life. My mom and dad are pretty good proof that she's right. Some days they have so many mood swings, we could put in a playground.

MOOD SWINGS

SNIDE

GAME WHERE YOU JUST SCREAM AT EACH OTHER

Friday, we're doing something for Aunt Carol's wedding at my house. The main reason is to torture me with the gruesome poofy brown bridesmaids' dresses and wooden clogs that we are being forced to wear as bridesmaids. Thanks for that, Isabella.

By the way, do you know how bridesmaids got the name **BRIDESMAIDS**? It was like this:

It's hard not to blame Angeline for all of this, since she IS somebody other than myself. But it's really kind of Isabella's doing, since she tricked Aunt Carol into thinking brown poofy dresses and **CLOGS** were the coolest things you could accessorize your wedding with.

But it's very hard for me to blame Isabella for anything, even when somebody shows me photographic evidence.

And besides, Angeline is much prettier and therefore more **blamelicious**.

my mom took this photo. She says Isabella pushed me into the lake, but I think she was trying to catch me.

# Tuesday 03

Dear Dumb Diary,

Margaret is on the dance committee, which is weird because she is one of those oafish people that you just naturally assume dances like somebody slipped a ferret down her pants. She's not totally a girl, not totally an ape. She's what you might call a **girlilla**.

GIRL

APE

GIRLILLA

The dance is at the end of the month, but it takes **weeks** to magically transform our gym into a magnificent fairy-tale ballroom that looks just like a gym with some balloons in it.

Margaret asked me to help with the posters (my glitter skills are legendary) and I agreed to make one.

She wanted, like, a *JILLION* different posters, but *glitterizing* takes a long time, and I'm not going to ruin my reputation with a bunch of posters that start developing glitter bald-spots because I rushed it. (**The first rule of the road is that beautiful things take time, and you can't rush glue.**)

IF DA VINCI HAD BEEN MORE PATIENT WITH HIS GLITTER, MONA LISA COULD BE WAY TOTALLY CUTER.

I was going to suggest that she do a few herself, but because Margaret is a pencil chewer, making posters is probably impossible for her. When she sees all those delicious writing implements spread out in front of her, she'll feel like she's at a buffet.

So somebody else **HAS** to make posters. Posters are a critical part of the event because they help the boys start planning weeks in advance who they will want to ask to dance but won't.

They also help the girls plan who they will want to ask them to dance but will say no to if they do.

BOY
CLUSTER

GIRL
WAD

INVISIBLE
WALL
OF PURE
COWARDICE

Although I'm a legend at this glitterfication, I have to give Miss Anderson some credit for how awesome my glitter abilities are.

Miss Anderson is my art teacher, and **BTF**, which is like a **BFF** except that the object is a teacher. But even though she is merely a teacher, she rarely wears teacher clothes and is beautiful enough to be a waitress, or maybe even a weather lady. She tried to steal Uncle Assistant Principal Devon away from my Aunt Carol when they first started dating, so Aunt Carol probably hates her at least forever and maybe longer.

Everybody knows that Miss Anderson is a **Total Master of All Things Sparkly** and taught me some of her amazing **twinklization techniques**, which are so excellent they can only be called **Glitter-Fu**.

Since Aunt Carol hates Miss Anderson, I never say anything nice about her in Aunt Carol's presence, which is **The Rule** you're supposed to observe when dealing with people who have intense feelings about things.

Like, you would never go on and on to a mouse about how wonderful cats are, or tell your friend, Mr. Snowman, about how much you're looking forward to summer, or tell Miss Bruntford (the cafeteria lady) how sensible it is to not eat nine or ten pies a day.

IF SHE ATE LESS PIE, BRUNTFORD COULD BE SKINNY AS A TOOTHPICK. (FACTORY)

I think Aunt Carol is over it all now, anyway, because I heard her say they were inviting all of the teachers to the wedding, even "**Miss Arty-Farty**," which I'm almost certain is Aunt Carol's code name for Miss Anderson — and is better than the other one she had for her, which was just a long string of screamy swear words.

# Wednesday 04

Dear Dumb Diary,

    Stinker ate a jar of my glitter.

    Right after school I started on my poster. I use shaker tops on my glitter jars. When Stinker saw me shaking one, he must have thought it was some sort of delicious seasoning, because when I turned my back for just a second, he managed to gnaw the top off my sparkling gold and ate the entire jarful.

THE HOG DOG

I think the glitter made him feel a little dizzy because he was walking all wobbly and bumped into the wall. Although it could have been partially caused by me trying to shake the glitter directly out of his face and onto my poster.

Now my arms hurt because Stinker would be considered fat even if he had been born as three dogs. But it gave me a great idea for a health club where you build up your muscles by hoisting chubbier and chubbier dogs.

NEED A SPOT?

# Thursday 05

Dear Dumb Diary,

　　Mom said Stinker was acting all weird so we had to take him to the veterinarian after school to make sure he doesn't have *Twinkle Poisoning* or *Sparklititis* or whatever eating a jar of glitter would do to you.

　　Isabella came with us because she really wants a puppy and her mom won't let her have one because Isabella has had some really bad luck with pets.

MISSY RAN AWAY

CUPCAKE RAN AWAY

DOODLE, WEE WEE, TAFFY, AND FUZZY RAN AWAY

BOBO CURRENTLY RUNNING AWAY BUT ONLY GETS A FEW INCHES A DAY

Isabella was hoping that if the vet was handing out free samples in the form of puppies and she just showed up at home with one, her mom wouldn't be able to say no. Since looking directly into a puppy's eyes and telling it that you don't love it is a scientific impossibility.

Unfortunately, there was no puppy giveaway, and even more unfortunately, guess who we ran into? Angeline and her mom.

And guess who had to *totally copy me* and get a dog? That's right: Angeline. And as if copying me wasn't bad enough, she's also copying about *50 million* other dog owners in America, which has to make this one of the worst cases of copying ever documented.

Entire NATION MAD AT ANGELINE FOR COPYING THEIR DOGS

Just to show off, Angeline couldn't get a regular dog, she had to go and get a **RESCUE DOG**.

A rescue dog is one of those dogs at the pound that nobody wants. They're usually not puppies, but they are cute, smart dogs that need a home. (Although if I was a dog and had to choose between the pound and Angeline, I would choose the pound, unless the third choice was to pound Angeline.)

Even though Angeline's rescue dog came with an adorable name (her name is *Stickybuns*), she is fortunately *unlike* most rescue dogs in that she is powerfully ugly and has some brain damage. I diagnosed it when she wasn't sickened after Stinker licked her face, which, put in people terms, would be like if . . . well, it would be like if Stinker licked your people face.

How YICKY IS THIS?

Even though Stickybuns is gross and dumb, Isabella was super jealous of Angeline's dog. You could tell because she was looking not at all jealous, which is an even jealouser way to look than plain old jealous. Isabella is a master of cover-ups. And when I said maybe her mom would let her get a rescue dog, she said that she wants a puppy. And then she spelled puppy for me a couple times, which is how I know she was upset because that's the only time people spell words at you.

The vet checked Stinker over and said that he looked fine, which I think means he looks fine for a dog-shaped balloon full of glitter and foulness.

But honestly, I wasn't really listening. The hideousness of Angeline's dog had put me in a really good mood and I just wanted to get back to my poster and leave Angeline and her Stickybuns behind.

**3** MORE THINGS THAT PUT ME IN A GOOD MOOD

**1.** JOLLY OLD SANTA!

**2.** SANTA GOES ZOMBIE AND EATS ANGELINE'S ARM OFF.

**3.** ACTUALLY ZOMBIE SANTA SCARES ME A LITTLE AND I HAVE TO GO LOCK MY WINDOWS NOW.

# Friday 06

Dear Dumb Diary,

Aunt Carol, Uncle Dan, Isabella, and Angeline came over tonight, just as had been earlier threatened.

Isabella and I have been trying to wear these dumb clogs that Aunt Carol gave us. Her advice was to wear them a little bit every day because that way we'd get used to them. Evidently, crying bridesmaids with bleeding feet are one of the main symptoms of a wedding that isn't going well.

Other symptoms include:

1. After bride says "I do," she follows it up with "Yeah, right."
2. Groom bites head off bride cake-topper.
3. Bride's eleven ex-husbands show up for ceremony.
4. Wedding rings. Onion rings. What's the diff?
5. When groom is told he may kiss the bride, he says "I'll pass."

6. Instead of throwing her bouquet, Bride makes groom EAT IT.

Angeline brought Stickybuns over to my house for this Bridesmaid Fashion Show. She **SAID** it was because the dog is still a little nervous and doesn't like to be left alone, but I'm sure it was really to show off that she has used her horrible **beauty-voodoo** to transform Stickybuns into what might be the *Cutest Dog in the State*.

Pretty girls can really do this. Isabella says it's an evil Black Magic that's called Pink Magic.

WHAT GIRLS WHO PRACTICE
PINK MAGIC CAN DO...

MAKE UNICORNS OBEY THEM

MAKE THEIR FACES BREAK OUT IN MAKEUP

MAKE PEOPLE PUT THEM IN THE WORST MOVIES YOU'VE EVER SEEN

Isabella suggested that we put Stickybuns in the backyard with Stinker, which I thought was a great idea because associating with Stinker could only ugly her up. Ugly dogs really can do this and I think it should be called Brown Magic.

Isabella and I went up to my room to change, and I started complaining about the clogs and how we should just refuse to wear them. But she very calmly said, "**Don't even bother putting them on,**" and walked out of my room.

CLOG

CLOG

Face it. This shoe was named after a disgusting plug of HAIR AND toothpaste-spit.

The next thing I heard was a terrible scream and a crash and then Isabella crying and wailing like somebody was slowly cutting her in half with those kindergarten scissors that can hardly even cut paper in half, much less an Isabella. When I came charging out of my room, I saw that she had fallen down the stairs.

OMG! MY BFF DOA??

Everybody was gathered around her at the bottom of the stairs, and she was moaning and sobbing so hard that she couldn't answer when they asked her what happened. Finally, Angeline asked, "Was it the clogs? Did the clogs make you fall?"

Isabella just buried her face in her hands and cried harder.

"It was the clogs," Angeline said softly, like a professional doctor. "She just doesn't want to say it. She doesn't want to hurt Aunt Carol's feelings. But it was the clogs."

Two minutes later, Aunt Carol was telling us that we could wear different shoes, and not to worry about it, everything would be fine. The adults were all taking turns feeding Isabella spoonfuls of ice cream and gently smoothing her hair to calm her down because for some reason when we're upset everybody assumes we want flatter hair.

Ten minutes and two bowls of ice cream later, Isabella and I were back up in my room. She was still sobbing a little when Angeline came in to hand us the dresses.

"Very clever, Isabella," Angeline said, and Isabella's sobs turned into a laugh, which was alarming. When Isabella laughs like that, often something very bad is about to happen to you. I always immediately look behind me to make sure I'm not about to back into an airplane propeller or something like that.

I'm afraid one day it will be something like this

But she was laughing about her little **trick**. Isabella threw herself down the stairs *on purpose*. Turns out that a fake tumble down the stairs is just another thing Isabella has mastered in order to get her mean older brothers in trouble.

More of Her BROTHER-Troubling Skills

CAN ARTFULLY BEND HeR GLASSES TO LOOK LIKE HeR BROTHeRS BROKe THeM.

CAN USe KETCHUP TO TOTALLY SIMULATE A **CUT LIP.**

CAN PUNCH HERSELF A BRUISe IN THE MIDDLE OF HeR OWN BACK.
(ONLY KNOWN HUMAN THAT CAN)

"I almost pretended to choke to death on the ice cream so that they'd go get me something better," she said. "But the **Choking to Death Routine** takes a lot of work to do correctly, and I just want to get this bridesmaid fashion show over with."

I've seen the CHOKING TO DEATH thing.

She can even DO it STANDING UP.

Once Isabella had spent a few minutes faking a recovery, we tried on the **DRESSES**. The dresses are too ugly to be described by the human mouth or drawn by the human pen. They're **POOFY**, big, and the exact same color of brown that delicious things never are.

Aunt Carol also brought over a bunch of big sparkly earrings, glittery necklaces, and other jewelry like that for us to try on, but none of it helped much — which tells you how awful these dresses are. A big pair of sparkly earrings and a necklace can save just about any outfit.

BEFORE

AFTER

BELLY BUTTON RING

More than anything, I looked like a spat-out lump of gristle wadded up in a napkin. And just when I thought it could get no more awful, it got awfuller.

Isabella didn't look half bad.

The poofs actually seemed to be working for her. They puffed where they should puff. They fluffed where they should fluff. If I hadn't looked like a jellyfish that had swallowed a full diaper, I might have even been happy for her.

Isabella
RUDELY
NOT LOOKING
HORRIBLE

But my mom was calling us to come downstairs and model them. All I could do was beg Isabella to fall again but she wouldn't. "Forget it," she said, "I like this dress."

So I pushed my best friend down the stairs.

Actually, it turns out that Isabella's mean older brothers have made her pretty instinctive about when somebody is about to push her down the stairs. She stepped out of the way as nimbly as a bullfighter, sending me bouncing down the stairs face-first.

Normally, this would have made me cry and Isabella laugh, but Angeline was already downstairs modeling her dress and none of us could do anything but stare at Angeline.

THUMP
THUMP
THUMP
THUMP
THUMP
THUMP
THUMP THUD

I might have even been knocked out for a minute, because I kind of remember a dream or a vision or something. It was long ago. All these cave people gathered together because some caveman invented a solid-gold violin or something. They just stood there, listening to the music, trying to understand how beautiful the pure beauty of this violin could be. And they oinked and scratched their butts and grunted about how great solid-gold violins are and said things like, "Don't we all wish we had invented them?" and other cave people stuff like that.

So do you understand the dream, Dumb Diary? Angeline was the solid-gold violin. Everybody else was a cave person. I was something smeared on the bottom of a caveman's foot.

All of this would have been bad enough, but as the cave people discussed the little alterations they needed to make here and there, I saw the disappointment in the eyes of Uncle Assistant Principal Devon when he looked at me, his future niece, standing there looking utterly *craptastic*.

The torture just seemed to go on and on forever. I was so glad when they gathered up all the bridesmaids' stuff, including Stickybuns, and left.

Looking
AT me
WITH
TOTAL
DISAPPOINTMENT

ANGELINE
(DRAMATICALLY
OUT OF FOCUS)

# Saturday 07

Dear Dumb Diary,

This morning I found a big pair of sparkly earrings in the yard, which must have dropped off Angeline when she went out to get Stickybuns. I guess her earlobes just aren't well developed enough to support jewelry.

I'll give them back to Aunt Carol on Monday.

Suffering from the SHAME of INADEQUATE LOBES

LOBE ADEQUACY MIGHT BE MY NEW FAVORITE WAY TO JUDGE PEOPLE

Margaret called this afternoon to bug me about hurrying up and finishing my poster. Margaret is a **HIGHLY CONTAGIOUS WORRIER** and she managed to infect me over the phone.

I started worrying about the dance. It's only, like, three weeks away, and I really have to practice standing.

I know, Dumb Diary, you might think that since it's a dance I need to practice dancing. But dancing is easy. I know how to dance.

## FAMOUS STANDS

"GALBILLY"

"MISS MYSTERY"

The problem is that there is **A LOT** of standing around at a dance, and I need to make sure I get my various standing moves perfect. I called Isabella to come over and help me but she got into some kind of trouble when she got home from my house last night, and she's waiting to find out what her punishment is going to be.

"BORED BORED BORED"

"I'M A MOOSE" (rarely used)

"I'M LAUGHING AT SOMETHING. IS IT YOU? YES, PROBABLY."

I started worrying about how my disappointed Uncle Assistant Principal Devon will behave at the dance. (Chaperoning dances is one of his official duties, along with telling us not to run in the halls and seeing how many times in a year a man can wear the same necktie.)

And that made me worry about how gross I'm going to look at the wedding, and what if I stand wrong at the dance? As I began to work on my poster, I felt the throb of a stress pimple suddenly begin deep under the skin of my chin.

The Zit Fairy

It doesn't show yet, but now that I'm the expectant mother of a new pimple, I have to deal with all of the things a new pimple-parent has to deal with.

My pimple, like any youngster, is going to need a lot of attention. I have to spend the time every day letting it know how much I resent it. I think that's really the most important part of pimple-parenting: letting your pimple know how much you hate it.

Even though it's sore, it's still super-tiny —
and thankfully nobody on Earth could ever detect
it yet.

BEFORE
PIMPLE →

WITH
PIMPLE →

# Sunday 08

Dear Dumb Diary,

Isabella came over today and from about eight houses away she detected the emerging pimple.

"Pimple, huh? When do you think it's due?" she said.

ME

SUPER HUMILIATION VISION

I wanted to deny it, but Isabella is quite skilled at identifying blemishes. Sadly, she can never put this strong natural talent to use as a dermatologist, since her urge to make fun of blemishes is even stronger than her ability to spot them. She says that her patients with acne would probably be big babies about being called names like "Pizza Face."

There was no keeping the truth from Isabella. She looked closely at my chin and said, "Hi, Fred."

"Who are you talking to?" I said. "Who's Fred?"

"I always name your pimples," she said. "This one looks like a Fred to me. Probably stress, huh? Because you stand dumb and you look awful in the bridesmaid's dress?"

**"YOU NAME MY PIMPLES?"** I yelled.

And she said, like it was perfectly normal, "Sure. They're like my little pets. They show up, I name them and watch them grow, and then they go away. Just like a real pet."

I hardly knew what to say. Isabella had been using my face as a day care.

"Hey," she said smiling, "remember the twins, Bumpo and Lumpo? They grew up so fast."

Isabella, the GROSSEST NANNY IN The WORLD

Then we got in a huge argument about dresses and pimples and whose butt resembles what when they dance and how some people should maybe just shut up.

This led to more talk about shutting up: specifically, who should do it and when. Then Isabella remembered that she should get off my property because I reminded her of it at the top of my lungs.

We BATTLED AS FiERCELY AS WOMEN BARBARIANS OR EVEN LADY GOLFERS

I hate it when Isabella and I fight.

All I want to do is finish my poster, sing my pimple a hateful little lullaby, and go to bed.

OTHER THINGS I DO AFTER WE FIGHT

EAT HALF GALLON OF ICE CREAM LIKE A HOG

FPOO

MAKE PAPER DOLL OF ISABELLA, BITE TO PIECES.

ACTUALLY, I DO THAT ICE CREAM HOG THING ALL THE TIME.

# Monday 09

Dear Dumb Diary,

This morning I was hanging up my poster at school, when Angeline arrogantly stopped to help me. She probably thought she was going to get credit for my glitter work.

Just as I finished getting it taped up, she looked over my shoulder, whipped something out of her purse, and smeared it across my chin.

SMEAR

I staggered back and flailed like a smeared poisoned person because I naturally assumed that it was some sort of poison she had smeared on me (out of jealousy for my awesome poster). Then I bumped directly into Hudson Rivers — eighth-cutest guy in my grade — who was right behind me.

Now that I think about it, even though I did it with my clumsy back, that totally counts as a hug.

I'LL BET JULIET BACKHUGGED ROMEO IN A SIMILAR OAFISHLY PRETTY WAY

And here's what he said — I'll remember it forever.

He looked right into my beautiful eyes and gently said, "**Walk much?**"

Okay, maybe that wasn't very nice, but then he got nicer right away.

"My mom is taking a few of us for tacos after the dance, if you two would like to come. But not Isabella. She can't come."

"We'd love it," I said quickly, not giving Angeline the opportunity to use the word **LOVE** in a sentence to Hudson, whom I had recently *backhugged*.

Cupid Bears The Cherished Tacos of Devotion and a medium Coke

As Hudson walked away, I suddenly remembered the poison that Angeline had used on me. "What did you wipe on my chin?" I demanded.

"I saw Hudson coming. It was some makeup to hide that bruise on your chin."

"It's a pimple," I medically informed her. "I'm going to give birth to a pimple."

"It's a bruise." she said, and tossed me the compact. "You probably got it when you slid down the stairs. It'll be gone in a couple days. You can keep the makeup."

ANGER STEAM

This is the exact moment when Isabella walked up. "Hey. How's little Fred coming along?" she asked.

And our fight was on again. It wasn't a full-length fight; it was just a micro-fight (a micro-fight lasts thirty seconds or less). Good friends know how to fight in a hurry. There's no telling how soon the two of us will have to gang up on somebody else, and let's face it, we both know the fight won't last forever, so why drag it out?

We made up really fast, and since we really hadn't officially made up from our fight before, we made up for that one, too.

So, as of **RIGHT THAT MINUTE**, Isabella and I were **BFFs** again, but let the record show that when I accepted Hudson's **TACOS OF DEVOTION** invitation, Isabella and I had not made up *YET*, so at that moment we **WEREN'T BFFs**, so technically speaking, I didn't *really* violate any of the **BEST FRIEND** rules.

THE RULES HAVE BEEN HANDED DOWN FOR CENTURIES.

THOU SHALT NOT ACCEPT INVITATIONS TO THINGS YOUR BFF IS NOT INVITED TO.

THOU SHALT NOT MAKE FUN OF YOUR BFF'S OUTFIT EVEN IF IT IS SUPER LAME.

THOU SHALT KEEP FIGHTS SHORT EVEN WHEN YOUR BFF IS TOTALLY BEING A HUGE DUMB JERK.

THOU SHALT SHARE YOUR STUFF WITH YOUR BFF BUT MAYBE NOT GUM IF YOU ARE WAY INTO GUM AND IT'S YOUR LAST PIECE.

And by the end of school, Isabella and I were totally friends again as if nothing had ever happened. We went by the school office to drop off the earrings with Aunt Carol. She wasn't there, so I left them in a bag on her desk.

I don't know why I always forgive Isabella, but I always do and I think I always will.

Forgiveness I've given Isabella...

MARKER ON FACE DURING SLEEPOVER (LAST YEAR)

TOLD ME SHE HAD DEADLY DISEASE THAT COULD ONLY BE CURED BY CUPCAKES (2ND Grade)

DRESSED AS ME FOR HALLOWEEN (TWO TIMES)

# Tuesday 10

Dear Dumb Diary,

Angeline was stupidly right. I wasn't expecting a pimple. I was bruised. The sensation faded and it's clear to me now that it was not one of those underground volcano zits after all.

However, it can't be stressed enough that Rightness and Wrongness seem about the same when performed by people you can't stand. So all of you people out there that we don't like, take note of this: Whether you're Right or Wrong, we're just going to treat it like you're Wrong. So don't bother working too hard to get it Right.

WRONG          WRONGER

My science teacher, Mrs. Palmer, gave us an assignment today to create a diorama of a great moment in discovery, like when the minivan or gravity was invented.

A diorama, Dumb Diary, is basically a shoe box in which you glue things and then you get a **B**.

There's more to it than that, but don't ask Mike Pinsetti to explain. The last shoe box diorama he did still had the shoes in it.

And why do Teachers WANT
our shoebox DIORAMAS anyway?

Coffee MoAT

They're probably
Building some sort
of TEACHER
FORTRESS to
grade PAPERS
AND DRINK
COFFEE AND BORE
each other IN.

Isabella came over tonight after dinner to **"WORK ON OUR DISCOVERY DIORAMAS."** I put those little quotation marks around that phrase to indicate that we only *said* that's what we were going to do. What we really wanted to do was practice standing for the dance.

I wonder why quotation marks mean that you're lying when you use them like that. Maybe it's because the lie is a huge load of stinking garbage, and the quotation marks are supposed to look like little flies buzzing around it.

Isabella worked really hard to help me figure out some good ways to stand at the dance. I think I've mastered three important stands:

1. Standing here, but moving just enough to prove that I'm into music.

2. Bored, but oh my gosh, I'm so cutely bored.

3. Standing here, but anybody can tell I've got cooler things to do. I mean, come on.

Isabella has mastered a couple of stands that very few people pull off. For instance:

1. Why don't you come over here and I'll make you eat one of your own shoes?

2. I'm cute, but in the way a porcupine holding a match and a stick of dynamite is cute.

3. I love this song, so unless you feel like meeting a paramedic soon, I wouldn't interrupt me right now.

Isabella helped me so much with my standing that I feel **totally, totally, totally, totally, totally, totally, totally, totally, totally,** *totally* terrible about ditching her for tacos with Hudson.

But hey! What do you know? Now I don't. Wow, I got over that fast. You'd think a person would take longer to recover from ten totallys. Guess I'm just a strong person.

PLUS I'M REALLY SWEET.

I'm like a very MUSCULAR BUNNY.

# Wednesday 11

Dear Dumb Diary,

OH, MAN! Right in the middle of art class today, Uncle Assistant Principal Devon and Aunt Carol came to the door and asked Miss Anderson to step out into the hall for a chat.

Aunt Carol looked so mean and angry that for a minute I almost thought she was my mom. My future uncle looked distressed and confused. After about two minutes the three of them were doing that sort of angry-whispery-private-talking that is a signal to others to drop everything and listen more closely.

A KNOWN SCIENCE FACT:

The more quietly people Argue, the Better your HEARING Becomes.

Isabella and I probably would have ignored it a little longer, except that Angeline started creeping toward the door to hear better, and we decided we'd better get up there with her to make sure she didn't violate their privacy more than was acceptable.

When we peeked around the doorway, we saw that Aunt Carol was waving the big glittery earrings I had left in a bag on her desk in Miss Anderson's face. Miss Anderson was saying that she had no idea what they were or where they came from, and Aunt Carol was saying it was obvious that Miss Anderson had left them there because everybody knows about her arty glitter thing and how she was never happy that Aunt Carol and Assistant Principal Devon were engaged, and who on Earth would put glitter on dog turds, anyway?

Glitter on Dog Turds. Glitter on Dog Turds. It echoed inside my head for a moment, and I started thinking, *It would be a really cool name for a band, but I'm not sure what their costumes would look like.* Then it suddenly occurred to me:

Those weren't big glittery earrings that Angeline dropped in my yard. The glitter that Stinker ate had finally made its way through his system. Those were sparkly Stinker doodies!

There's no easy way to jump into a situation like this. And that's why it was so easy to not do it.

We ran back to our seats and pretended like we had no idea what was making Miss Anderson so angry when she stormed back in and slammed the door behind her.

"Some people!" she said, and we all nodded because nodding is the wisest thing to do to an angry person.

## Things You Should NEVER Do Around An Angry Person

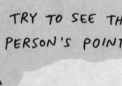

TRY TO SEE THE OTHER PERSON'S POINT OF VIEW.

LAUGH AT HOW HIGH-PITCHED THEIR VOICE GETS WHEN THEY SCREAM.

BREATHE OR BLINK.

# Thursday 12

Dear Dumb Diary,

All night I worried about Miss Anderson. It didn't help that Isabella told me that turd-leaving is probably a Hygiene Crime. She told me about this one girl from another school who sneezed underneath one of those plastic sneeze guards at a salad bar and, as a penalty for her Hygiene Crime, the judge made her work at that restaurant for the rest of her life. I know exactly the really really old waitress she's talking about. She's one of those waitresses who's so old that you feel bad asking her to bring you your food. You want to tell her to sit down and you'll go get it.

I think those old waitresses deserve to retire. Maybe it's just because I'm so nice, but I always drop a note in their suggestion box that they should fire those old waitresses.

I woke up thinking that I should go tell Miss Anderson exactly what happened, but once I got to school, Isabella talked me out of it. She said that if I had to tell somebody I should tell my Aunt Carol, because then she could just call the police and have the charges dropped.

So I went to talk to Aunt Carol. I told her that I had left the sparkly poos on her desk and she got all teary-eyed — which she has been doing a **LOT** since she got engaged — and gave me this huge, gross slobbery hug.

"That's sweet of you to take the blame, Jamie. But Angeline already told us that she did it. She apologized. It turns out that it was a just a joke that went bad. We all hugged and made up. I even apologized to Miss Anderson.

"So it's all behind us now but, of course, after the blowup with Miss Anderson, Angeline had to be punished. So she doesn't get to go to the dance."

FIANCEES ARE AS WEEPY AS BABIES

BUT THEIR ARMS ARE AS STRONG AS BIGFOOT'S

Angeline doesn't get to go to the dance? And if she doesn't go to the dance, she can't go for tacos after the dance! This is all my fault.

It's hard to believe sometimes just how great my fault can make things turn out.

## ☆ FAULTGIRL ☆
### SAVING THE DAY THROUGH HER CARELESSNESS!

ONE DAY...

SHE LEAVES THE LIGHTS ON IN HER ROOM WHICH CAUSES **GLOBAL WARMING.**

AND THE MELTING POLAR ICE CAPS *CHANGE EARTH'S ORBIT!*

THIS CAUSES THE PLANET TO MOVE DIRECTLY INTO THE PATH OF A SPEEDING ASTEROID!!!

WHICH HITS ANGELINE RIGHT IN THE HAIR.

# FRIDAY 13

Dear Dumb Diary,

Isabella came over today. She needed to take Stinker for a walk because she says that she's doing her Discovery Diorama on Baron Von Leash — who is the guy that invented the leash — and she has to make some notes on leashes. I wish I could come up with a topic that good.

Before they left on their little stroll, I asked Isabella why Angeline would confess to the "DOG EARRINGS" I left on Aunt Carol's desk (note those little flies buzzing around the words *dog earrings*).

Isabella had a pretty good theory. She thinks it's because Angeline is super-dumb.

SCIENTIST ISABELLA EXAMINES A MOLECULE OF SUPER-DUMBNESS extracted from Angeline

Isabella is probably right. She almost always is.

When I think back on all the things I've seen Angeline do, the one thing they have in common is that they're all dumb. (They're all strawberry-scented, too, but I think that's just her conditioner — although her body might actually secrete its own strawberry scent.)

But of all the dumb things she's ever done, taking the blame when she didn't actually drop a doggy-deuce on my aunt's desk has to rate as one of the dumbest.

HER HAIR PROBABLY GOES ALL THE WAY INTO HER HEAD LIKE A DOLL'S

Although I'm not sure Isabella should be talking about dumbness. She and Stinker were gone for an hour and a half because she got lost in the neighborhood. Plus, she doesn't even know how to take care of a dog. Stinker came back more scruffy and dirty than usual.

BEFORE

AFTER

# Saturday 14

Dear Dumb Diary,

    First thing this morning, my mom told me that Aunt Carol was taking Angeline, Isabella, and me out to buy shoes to replace the clogs.
    Normally, I like shopping for shoes, but I knew I would have to look Angeline directly in her face, which wouldn't be going to the dance.

Actually, None of HeR is...

We picked up Angeline at her house, and when we got there, she was sitting outside brushing Stickybuns, who has gotten even prettier: Angeline's evil beautification skills at work.

Isabella is obviously still jealous of Stickybuns: She was staring at the dog so long it barked at her.

Isabella still thinks that Angeline might be super-dumb. She immediately started talking very slowly to Angeline, like she was two years old or something. She says that's how you have to talk to people who are as dumb as Angeline.

It seemed to bother Angeline quite a bit, but Isabella says that people that dumb anger easily, like when they aren't allowed to have a fifth helping of pudding, or when somebody misplaces their chew toy.

We tried on a lot of shoes.

We tried on some of those ones with really pointy toes that would be handy if you wanted to shish kebab something while looking elegant.

We tried on some really flat ones that would be perfect if the look you were going for was a ballerina that doesn't have any other kind of shoe to wear except those blunt slippers that make you look shorter than you actually are.

We tried on some of those shoes that restrain you with a lot of straps that also make it look like maybe your foot is a dangerous animal that you're concerned might escape.

SHOEMAKERS OFTEN DARE EACH OTHER TO MAKE THE UGLIEST SHOE IN THE WORLD.

Finally, Aunt Carol decided on some brown shoes with medium-high heels. This came after we determined that only Angeline was disproportioned enough to walk in the high-high heels.

Later, when we dropped Angeline off at home, she reminded us to make sure to wear the shoes around to get used to them.

And Isabella told her that was a good idea, but if you're going to walk around in the yard, be careful not to step in any earrings — which was a totally stupid thing to say. As we were pulling away, I looked back and saw Angeline putting it all together in her head.

I told Isabella that Angeline is not as dumb as we hope she'll look one day.

Isabella says not to worry about it. Since it wasn't me who said it, Angeline must think Isabella left the doggy-doo on Aunt Carol's desk.

Isabella says that the simple rule of guilt is this: *You feel less guilty when people don't know you are.*

Some things are Best when ignored.

Like Guilt!

# Sunday 15

Dear Dumb Diary,

Sunday is homework day, so Isabella came over to walk Stinker again. She said she misplaced the notes that she made last time. (And get this: She got lost again, and Stinker returned all dirty and scruffed up again.)

While they were out, I spent about two hours in my room looking for a book I got from the library about inventors. Mom always tells me that I should be more organized, but I think that organization is for people who are just too lazy to spend two hours looking for something.

I have an old Barbie that I thought would look good in my diorama, but I couldn't find any inventors who looked like her. Evidently, seven-foot-tall blond girls are in short supply in the science department.

There was one inventor lady who looked a little like a Mr. Potato Head, but Stinker ate all the parts from my Mr. Potato Head years ago, so now he's just Mr. Potato with Face Wounds, and too disturbing for a diorama.

She won't even fit in A SHOEBOX.

OH, BARBIE you're just TOO Leggy foR Science.

The Barbie reminded me a little of Angeline, and I found myself acting out a little scene in which she's watching me and Hudson drive away for tacos, and she's crying and crying because she doesn't even get to go to the dance, and I suddenly realized something.

I realized I love live theater.

I'M WAAAAY TOO OLD TO PLAY WITH DOLLS, BUT THIS WAS ODDLY SATISFYING

I also realized that it wasn't Angeline's fault that she was going to feel so bad. It was Isabella's fault for cluing her in.

And it was Hudson's fault for asking us to taco-eating and not Isabella.

And it was America's fault for encouraging middle schools to have dances.

It amazes me sometimes, how anybody could ever think anything was my fault.

PLUS SINCE MY MOM MANUFACTURED ME

DOESN'T THAT MAKE EVERYTHING I DO HER FAULT?

Anyway, I don't want to think about it now. I'm going to go back to reading about inventors.

# Monday 16

Dear Dumb Diary,

Aunt Carol's wedding has also made Mom a little bit insane. Dad keeps saying that weddings can make everybody associated with them crazy, and now I think he could be right. She keeps going on and on about how happy she is that this person or that person will be at the wedding.

I'm really not looking forward to seeing people I haven't seen in a long time because of the inevitable conversation that will follow:

**OLD GASBAG RELATIVE:** Oh, hello, Janey.

**ME:** It's Jamie.

**OLD GASBAG RELATIVE:** Oh, that's right. My goodness, you sure have grown.

**ME:** Grown what?

**OLD GASBAG RELATIVE:** Flarby flurb dee flub.

(Old Gasbag won't *really* say that last line, but by this time I will be facedown asleep in my dinner and that's what it will sound like to me.)

After she was done chirping about the wedding for a while, Mom got all smiley and squeaky and started talking about me maybe having a new little cousin to cuddle and kiss pretty soon.

At first I thought she meant Angeline, and I became so psychologically freaked out that I fainted a little. While Dad was getting ready to call the hospital, Mom said that she meant that Aunt Carol and Uncle Assistant Principal Devon might have a baby one day, and **THAT** would be my new kissy cousin.

The thought ALMOST MADE ME INSANE FOREVER

Then she explained that Angeline and I won't be cousins. When your aunt marries somebody else's uncle, it doesn't make you related. **NOT AT ALL.** **DID YOU HEAR THAT, DUMB DIARY? NOT RELATED. NOT AT ALL.**

IT'S LIKE HAVING A LARGE, VERY ATTRACTIVE WART REMOVED

This is the best Angeline-related news I had heard since that one time we thought she had head lice. (Sadly, it turned out to be nothing more than some butterflies that had been attracted to her pleasant scent.)

Now don't get me wrong, Angeline did **NOT** crumble into a little pile of dust, so this isn't like Santa answered my last four letters or anything. But still, **This Is Really Good News!**

# Tuesday 17

Dear Dumb Diary,

    Today in science, Mrs. Palmer taught us about a few of the **Great Moments in Science** that were so great and momentous and significant to humankind that they might deserve to be depicted inside an old shoe box.

Like, long ago, there was this one person who decided that she was tired of walking everywhere. So she caught a horse, saddled it, and forced it to take her places.

After that, other people decided that horses weren't good enough. They decided to force dirt to turn into steel so they could bang it into cars, and then pump oil out of the ground to run the cars so that the cars could take them places.

And now there are people who think that cars aren't environmental enough, and they plan to build machines to turn corn into fuel that will power the cars to take us places.

I raised my hand and pointed out that we could just feed the corn to the horses and solve a few of our problems right there.

But here's the thing, Dumb Diary. Teachers SAY that they want you to participate and be clever, but you have to time it just right, or they think you're being a smart-mouth. Mrs. Palmer was right on the verge of making some BIG SCIENCE POINT. I must have broken her train of thought or something because she sent me on a made-up errand to the office to see if she had any mail.

I got there just in time to hear Aunt Carol and Uncle Assistant Principal Devon in his office shouting. I saw Aunt Carol come out and slam the door. I could tell she had been crying a little.

BIG GLIMMERY EYES LIKE A MANGA CHARACTER

PINK SNIFFLY NOSE

KLEENEX IN HAND

CRINKLY CHIN

I turned around and walked out of the office before she saw me, because I thought she would be embarrassed. Now I'm starting to think that Assistant Principal Devon is a rat.

I should probably not use the word *rat* like that because of its offensiveness to rats. If you are a real rat and reading this right now, no offense. Also, let go of my diary because — again, no offense — you really are a kind of horrible dirty filthy rodent. But congratulations on learning how to read!

Now drop my book.

# Wednesday 18

Dear Dumb Diary,

Isabella is becoming some kind of genius student. She is way into this report of hers on Baron Von Leash.

She came over **AGAIN** today to take Stinker for his walk. Stinker is really getting used to it because when he saw her he started jumping up and down. But he is so fat, he mostly jumps down.

As Isabella and Stinker were breezing out the door, I told her about Aunt Carol and Uncle Assistant Principal Devon to see if she would help me get the wedding canceled, but she said to forget it because she likes how she looks in the bridesmaid's dress.

Then, when I offered to go with her and Stinker so she wouldn't get lost **AGAIN,** she said no and that she probably **would** get lost again today so don't come looking for them if they don't come back for a while. And don't freak out if Stinker is all dirty and scruffy when they get back.

I wanted to tell Mom about Aunt Carol and Uncle Assistant Principal Devon, but she's too happy about this wedding. And since there are only four or five things that make moms happy, I couldn't bring myself to do it.

(The truth is, most things make moms angry.)

And **BTW** (that stands for By The Way), Isabella *did* get lost, and Stinker *was* all dirty and messed up again. It was just as she had amazingly predicted.

# Thursday 19

Dear Dumb Diary,

Isabella and I were eating lunch today. Meat loaf. Meat loaf is what they always do to us on Thursday.

Now don't get me wrong. Not all meat loaf is bad. Isabella's Mom makes this unbelievable meat loaf that is so delicious, it's probably the second best thing a cow could wish for. (Best thing cow could wish for: **NOT** being meat loaf.)

COW'S PLAN A

COW'S PLAN B

I was so focused on being intensely mad at Uncle Assistant Principal Devon for making my aunt cry, that eating good food would have been all wrong. The meat loaf was a perfect choice of dish to accompany that kind of rage.

Like, you know how there are some foods that, while you eat them, you just can't stay mad, like those ice-cream cones that they make to look like clowns? I couldn't stay mad if they gave us those for lunch. Nobody could.

Maybe for our next war, we should drop those on both sides.

Anyway, Aunt Carol and Uncle Assistant Principal Devon walked past our table, and Isabella decided to cleverly drop hints to them about the crying incident.

"Why were you crying in the office the other day?" she cleverly hinted. And the cleverness of her hint made me cleverly choke a little.

Isabella says there's nothing wrong with just BLURTING things out. She says that blurting is merely like kicking with your mouth.

Aunt Carol said, "Just nerves, Isabella. Weddings can do that to people. It was some silly thing I can't even remember now." Then she started to walk away, followed by Uncle Assistant Principal Devon.

Here's where I thought: *I see. It's all clear as can be. Okay, well, I guess we can drop it now.*

OK. It's over.

But as they turned to leave, Isabella grabbed Uncle Assistant Principal Devon's sleeve and added, like a person who was *not* dropping it now, "Good. Because I really want to wear that dress, even if Jamie hates hers."

Yup, cafeteria meat loaf was actually the **PERFECT** dish to go with today's conversation.

Luckily, Aunt Carol did not hear Isabella. I know, because Mom was not insane when I got home, and she would have been if Aunt Carol had called her with that little tidbit.

DADS GO INSANE, TOO. HERE'S A FEW EXAMPLES:

WHEN ADORABLE DAUGHTER FORGOT WHERE SHE BURIED THE T.V. REMOTE. AGAIN.

when trying to open and assemble toy.

when asked to form an opinion about drapes.

# Friday 20

Dear Dumb Diary,

When I got home, I found a big present on my bed from Aunt Carol. Evidently, there are a lot of presents given around weddings, and it's hard to argue with a policy like that while you're unwrapping one.

I AGREE WITH ME GETTING STUFF

Here's the note that came with it (I couldn't help but notice that she had placed the "flies" in the correct position):

Dear Jamie,
Thank you so much for being one of my bridesmaids. You, Angeline, and Isabella are going to make this such a special day for us!
Often the Bride gives her bridesmaids a piece of jewelry as a gift, but since we had that unpleasantness with the "earrings", your future Uncle Dan suggested dresses and shoes instead. (He even helped pick them out!) Can't wait to see you in them at the rehearsal.
Love,
Aunt Carol and Uncle Dan

Since the bridesmaid dresses are so *barftastic,* I was afraid of how this new dress was going to look on me, but incredibly, I looked pretty good in it. Aunt Carol had all my measurements, so it fit perfectly.

It's a really simple dress, and it's a deep chocolaty brown, like the way chocolate stuff looks on menus.

It was like something Miss Anderson would wear, and I have to admit that I looked better than pretty good in it. I looked much much better than pretty good. I looked beautiful and elegant at the same time, like if a chocolate rainbow and a chocolate chandelier had a baby.

I practiced the following beautiful moves in it:

BEAUTIFUL PETTING OF A BEAUTIFUL POODLE

BEAUTIFUL WAVING

BEAUTIFUL FOOD POISONING

I had it going on, Dumb Diary, and when we got to the restaurant for the rehearsal dinner, the going-on just kept on going. Isabella had the exact same outfit, but she didn't look any better than me. And even Angeline only looked much better, instead of much much much much much *much* better, which is how you would have expected Angeline to impolitely look.

THAT ANGELINE WAS PROBABLY CONFUSED SHE WAS NOT A JILLION TIMES PRETTIER THAN THE WHOLE WORLD

It turns out that a rehearsal is really just a nice dinner at which they tell us where to stand and where it is not okay to fart during the wedding.

Answer: On the bride's left.

Rehearsal dinners are usually held the night before the wedding, but they couldn't do it then. Because Uncle Assistant Principal Devon has to chaperone the dance. So we did it a week before.

Uncle Assistant Principal Devon had some of his friends there, who, surprisingly, are not teachers or other principals. I assumed that school people always hung out together, like buffalo or something.

These guys are his best man and groomsmen, and their job is to escort us down the aisle and hit anybody that makes fun of me in my bridesmaid's dress.

Right away I chose the biggest, ugliest groomsman because I figured he would make me look a little better.

The guests will be all like, "Wow, doesn't Jamie look only a little bit ghastly when compared to that Bigfoot who's walking her down the aisle?"

We also met Aunt Carol's maid of honor, Betsy. Suddenly, I realized exactly how those dresses were chosen: with Betsy's help.

Betsy is naturally shaped exactly like the bridesmaid's dress, and even her regular clothes had little bridesmaidy touches here and there.

People, we really need to work harder to put an end to **Frill Abuse**.

Betsy is kind of pink-faced all the time and giggles a lot. You can just tell she's one of those people who wraps presents with extra ribbon and has decorative soaps.

Betsy

Betsy's keys

All evening everybody went over all the wedding details. They went over and over everything.

It was all, "You walk in like this," and "You stand like that," and "Don't chew gum," and "Make sure you go to the bathroom first," and "Blah blah blah."

By the time we were done, I have to say I did **NOT** understand why people get married. There is just too much work involved.

I'm pretty sure that if they made divorces this complicated, more people would stay together out of pure laziness.

Here's how I think the **Divorce Ceremony** should go:

- You have to invite all the guests that were at the wedding, and they get their wedding presents back.

- At the end of the ceremony, instead of kissing, they bite each others' faces.

- Bridesmaids still have to wear gross dresses. (They make more sense here.)

# Saturday 21

Dear Dumb Diary,

    I was all prepared to not look beautiful today, but that didn't happen.
    I had totally forgotten that we had to go to Aunt Carol's bridal shower — which is another opportunity for the bride to delicately slobber up a bunch of extra presents before the wedding at which she'll slobber up a whole mountain of them.
    As it turns out, brides are so beautiful that just being around them can infect you with **Gorgeousness.** Before I knew it, I had to get all dolled up again.

A Bride moves her gifts with the traditional Matrimonial FoRK-Lift

They held the bridal shower over at Betsy's house (the maid of honor who is made of ruffles). Guess what? Her whole house looks like it's made out of bridesmaids' dresses.

It's like a **Museum of ADORABLENESS.** There are **DARLING** little lace doilies under everything and countless little statues of precious children and poodles with their heads cocked adorably. No matter what you think about Betsy, she is probably the world's total expert on **CUTENESS,** although that's a pretty dumb thing to be an expert on.

WUV YOU!

Of course, Angeline **HAD** to bring a photo of her little Stickybuns to show everybody. And yes, it **DID** have its head cocked like a professional ceramic statue, but I don't think we can rule out the possibility that Angeline held it in that position with tape and wire just for the photo.

CAUTION
LOOKING DIRECTLY AT THIS PICTURE COULD CAUSE CAVITIES

# Sunday 22

Dear Dumb Diary,

Isabella came by **AGAIN** to do some leash research with Stinker. I've never seen Stinker happier to see somebody. They were out for hours, and Stinker came back all dirty and scruffy again, but I guess that's the price he must pay for Education.

I haven't even figured out what to do my diorama about yet. I'm starting to worry that, next to Isabella's, mine is going to look less like a dio**RAMA** and more like a dio**REEYA**.

Me Being taken to an institution for people with A DIORAMA MAKING DISABILITY

I was glad that Isabella didn't hang around because I had to practice for my after-dance *Tacos of Devotion* with Hudson.

Like all normal people, I love tacos, but they are designed more to mouthfully enjoy than to appear lovely while eating. **In fact, there are five main foods** that were dumbly designed to lower your attractiveness while eating:

1. Popcorn (The only food eaten by packing entire mouth totally full before chewing.)
2. Watermelon (Lots of slobbery horking and spitting. The only food eaten the same way by monkeys and people.)

3. Spaghetti (Lots of slurping and leaning over plate in doglike posture. Occasional hair-in-sauce issues. Difficult not to look like animal eating shoelaces.)

4. Peel-and-eat shrimp (Lots of looking like you're eating world-record-sized bugs.)

5. Tacos (Lots of crippled-neck postures, and ingredients exploding everywhere. Can be noisy enough inside mouth to make hearing conversation difficult.)

Angeline would **NOT** have a problem with taco-eating. She could slurp a greasy tarantula out of an ash tray and make it look like she was eating a chocolate-covered strawberry.

But I have to practice, practice, practice.

We didn't have any taco shells in the house, so I just folded slices of toast and filled them with lettuce and corn flakes to represent **Basic Taco Anatomy.** I spent some time looking in a mirror and watching myself try to eat them without spewing ingredients everywhere or looking like I was missing my neckbones.

REAL LIFE TACO

SYNTHETIC PRACTICE TACO

At first, I wasn't sure I could eat them gracefully, but after some planning and a lot of practice, I finally realized that now I'm sure I can't do it gracefully.

I'm getting a burrito.

IT WAS KIND OF MESSY.

# Monday 23

Dear Dumb Diary,

So today, out of the blue, Isabella says to me, "Hey, Jamie. If one day some ugly tree in your backyard was covered with a whole bunch of ugly snakes, and your mom and dad didn't want them, you'd give one to me, right?"

The correct answer to this question is, of course, **"Yes."** Unless it's being asked by Isabella, in which case, experience has taught me to run all the way to the office and ask to phone home.

After ten minutes of begging, I finally got my mom to go outside and look for snakes. She said there were none and don't call home from school unless it's really important.

If Isabella says the words "snakes" and "in your backyard" in the same sentence, trust me: It's really important. But Mom doesn't know Isabella like I do, so she couldn't fully grasp the severity of the situation.

I always pay attention to whatever Isabella says

even if it's just something about TEDDY BEARS.

When I saw Isabella later, she asked me the question again and I told her that I didn't really understand why she would ask me about snakes in my yard.

"Okay. Let me rephrase the question," she said. "Let's say you bite into a burrito and a bunch of spiders crawl out. Would you let me have one?"

**OMG!** Does she know about the **Tacos of Devotion** I'm having with Hudson? Darn it, Isabella — **WE WEREN'T BFFS WHEN I ACCEPTED THE INVITATION!**

And now I can't even order a burrito.

# Tuesday 24

Dear Dumb Diary,

Today I saw Angeline tearing down my dance poster.

Of course, she **SAID** she was putting it back up because the tape had given out. She could have been telling the truth, I suppose, because my glitterwork **IS** robust.

She pointed at a little bare spot. "This could use a touch-up," she said. "Do you have any more of the gold glitter you used here?"

Does she know? **OMG! Sparkling Gold** is the name of the glitter in Stinker's "earrings." Is she toying with me?

IT'S THE GLITTER STINKER ATE !!!

# Wednesday 25

Dear Dumb Diary,

    I practiced taco-eating again today, even though I felt like I was a lost cause. Nothing short of a miracle was going to help me become a master taco eater.

    I set up my little pretend tacos in front of the mirror and thought long and hard about how I was going to do this. And when I went to take a bite, I spotted my cute self in the mirror — WITH MY HEAD COCKED.

It was a miracle! It was like a vision of Betsy came to me, and she was a chubby, bigheaded angel, wearing a poofy dress made of doilies and holding a bigheaded poodle puppy that was also an angel. They both had their heads cocked and they were both eating tacos.

I didn't really see this, but this is probably what I would have seen if I was a vision-having-type-person.

With my head in the pre-taco position, I looked exactly like one of Betsy's adorable little figurines. I made my eyes bigger and was suddenly so preciously cute and innocent that I almost pooped.

In that moment, just before I take a bite of taco, I am posed in the most adorable pose in the known universe. And even if the taco explodes into a cloud of ingredients, once I take a bite, the memory of my lovableness will linger.

I wish I played an instrument. That last sentence would be a really good song.

I suddenly realized that Betsy's Museum of Adorableness isn't so dumb after all. It stands as a shining example to all humanity of how you should hold your head to look cute.

See? IT WORKS FOR EVERYBODY!

# Thursday 26

Dear Dumb Diary,

    I had a horrible dream. I dreamed of Angeline — which is horrible all by itself — but it gets worse. We were at a taco restaurant, and Angeline was selling glittery jewelry for thousands of dollars. I was sitting there eating a taco, getting it all over my face, when Angeline walked over and gave me the money she'd made selling the jewelry. Then she took a napkin and wiped some taco sauce off my chin because she saw Hudson coming over to my table.

Angeline wiped the taco sauce off my chin, Dumb Diary! And I woke up screaming so loud, I wouldn't be surprised if Stinker made another set of earrings and maybe even a charm bracelet.

This dream is Angeline's fault. It was caused by Angeline putting her own makeup on my chin to save me a little embarrassment. Angeline's selfish niceness was cruelly making me feel guilty about letting her take the blame for the poo earrings. I couldn't keep it to myself any more — I had to confess!

the weight of the GUILT IS IMPOSSIBLE to BEAR

As soon as I got to school this morning, I told Uncle Assistant Principal Devon what happened. I explained everything to him. I told him how Stinker eats things all the time and they practically never come out looking like jewelry except for maybe the kind of jewelry you'd wear with those bridesmaids' dresses. Then I immediately regretted saying that because he got really quiet and serious and told me that I should have told him the truth right away.

They teach them poses like this at ASSISTANT PRINCIPAL SCHOOL

I told him that I thought that the truth was still the truth even if it's a couple days late. He thought about that for a minute and said, **"Dumbest thing I've ever heard."** Then he told me we would forget about the whole thing.

After that, I thought maybe he wasn't a rat.

He went on to say that Angeline *will* get to go the dance, which has me thinking again that he *is* a rat, because even if Angeline gets punished for something she didn't do, who would it hurt?

So I won't have Hudson all to myself over tacos tomorrow night. But if I can talk Angeline into getting the burrito, I'll still look adorable and she'll look like somebody trying to gag down a fire hose full of spiders.

NOTE: IT IS SCIENTIFICALLY IMPOSSIBLE to DRAW ANGELINE THAT GROSS.

SO HERE IS A PICTURE OF A KITTEN THAT IS WATCHING THE HORRIBLE DISPLAY

LATER, IT IS RUSHED TO THE HOSPITAL WHERE IT WILL REMAIN FOR SIX MONTHS.

# Friday 27

Dear Dumb Diary,

I just got back from the dance. Where should I start?

First of all, Angeline thanked me for telling Uncle Assistant Principal Devon the truth. Then she laughed at me for being dumb enough to mistake Stinker's creations for earrings.

I pointed out how dumb it was for her to take the blame for something she didn't do, and she said that she just did it so that Aunt Carol and Uncle Assistant Principal Devon would stop fussing over it.

She said that she totally knew that I had done it, but she really didn't care. She just wanted to make it stop. (I guess maybe she's not that dumb.)

I'll bet big Sparkly Doody Earrings are a HUGE FAD SOMEDAY

On the dancier side of things, the Dance Committee did a pretty good job of decorating the gym. They also picked really good music.

But here's how dumb Angeline is: She just starts dancing, and she's not doing it with anybody in particular. She just dances in every direction and she does it like nobody's watching. One minute she's dancing with Mike Pinsetti, and the next minute she's dancing with Margaret (who is a surprisingly good dancer and barely apelike).

It's so weird how easily dumbness comes to Angeline.

I think I probably had just as much fun standing still, and I only made a couple of mistakes, but I think I looked pretty good. Isabella and I both danced a little, but we didn't get all out of control like **Dancypants Angeline.**

it is very <u>rude</u> to dance much better than the people around you.

Uncle Assistant Principal Devon was there, even though the wedding is tomorrow. In spite of the fact that he is a rat, apparently he takes his principaling very seriously.

I couldn't totally enjoy the dance, because I was feeling bad about ditching Isabella the whole time. The **Taco Rendezvous** with Hudson was one of my dreams come true (below owning a talking unicorn, but above being able to talk to koalas).

When I looked at Isabella standing so professionally, I remembered back to the first really nice thing she did for me when we were kids.

We were in third grade, I think, and we were at lunch. I was eating some horrible thing that my mom had horribly packed for me, and Isabella had one of her mom's incredible meat loaf sandwiches. She looked over and saw how much I hated my lunch and then she did the sweetest thing you could imagine.

She pulled Eddy Dooley's hair until he gave me his lunch.

WASN'T TINY ISABELLA A CUTEY?

People don't always know how nice Isabella is or how she looks out for her **BFF**, but I do. And at that moment, I was overwhelmed with a dumb idea.

I told Angeline I wasn't going for tacos.

And she said, "I know. I knew you wouldn't ditch Isabella. It was mean of Hudson to say Isabella couldn't come, and I'm not going, either."

At the end of the dance, we told Hudson we weren't going. We didn't give him any reason. We just told him we weren't going.

Just as he was driving off into the night with his mom and a few other friends, Isabella caught up to us.

"Why aren't you two going for tacos?" she asked.

I was shocked. "You know about that?" I said.

"Of course I know about that."

Angeline was just as surprised. "Isabella," she said. "You should also know that Hudson invited us, but told us that you couldn't come."

Their van looked sad that I wasn't in it.

"That's right," Isabella said. "That's exactly what I told him two weeks ago. My mom won't let me go. When your Aunt Carol drove me home from your house a couple weeks ago, she came in and told my mom about my fall down the stairs. That fall may have fooled your family, Jamie, but the last time I successfully fooled my mom with that one I was four. She was mad that I did it at your house. She almost said I couldn't go to the dance at all, but she's not totally immune to my fake crying yet, so here I am.

"But when I told her that Hudson asked me to go for tacos after, she said I couldn't go, as a punishment. Hudson asked me *before* he asked you two. I told him I couldn't go."

"Jamie, I would have told you, but we were fighting that day. It just hasn't come up since."

I CAN'T GO

SHE CAN'T COME

He WAS just telling us what she told HIM

And then Isabella looked really confused. "But why didn't you two go?" she asked.

"I have no idea, Isabella," I said. "We decided not to go because we thought he was ditching you."

"That was pretty dumb," she said.

And she was right.

Like a DANGEROUS DUMB Rescue of somebody who isn't in trouble

# Saturday 28

Dear Dumb Diary,

Today was **"Aunt Carol's Big Day."**
It started out with a panicky phone call from
Aunt Carol. Uncle Assistant Principal Devon had
picked up the bridesmaids' dresses after they
were altered and left them in his unlocked car. Get
this: Somebody stole them, so we had to wear the
dresses we wore to the rehearsal dinner.
**STOLE THEM!** Maybe criminals aren't
all bad!

We don't say enough nice things
about horrible human beings like thieves

It worked out fine. We all looked great, even Betsy. Her dress wasn't stolen, since it didn't need to be altered and she had it at home. She still had all the precious adorablenesss she loves. And let's face it: The girl can work the ruffles.

*Betsy was MADE for MAIDING*

The teachers who came to the reception looked good, too, even Miss Bruntford. She had on a big flowery dress that kind of made her look like a couch standing up on its side. But still, a really nice couch.

Being an art teacher, Miss Anderson is an expert on good-lookingness, and today was no exception. Her dress, shoes, and lipstick were all laser-pointer red, and her fingernails looked like if Barbie turned into a werewolf.

But Aunt Carol, being the bride, was legally entitled to be the prettiest one there, and she was.

And even though it looked like they had crammed her into the wedding dress, she looked glamorously crammed.

The wedding ceremony itself was kind of boring and long. But that makes sense because the idea is to glue two people together forever and **the first rule of the road is that beautiful things take time, and you can't rush glue.**

The reception was a lot different from the ceremony. The food was pretty good, and there were no Old Gasbag Relatives quizzing me until I fell asleep in it.

It was really funny watching Aunt Carol and Uncle Assistant Principal Devon jam cake into each other's faces. I think that may be the one wedding tradition that could be carried over to the Divorce Ceremony.

I danced the dumb way that Angeline danced — in every direction and not caring who saw — and it was a lot more fun than standing. I may even do less standing at the next school dance.

Okay, I admit it

I'm a great DANCER

At some point during the night, I saw myself in a mirror in the hallway and was so grateful I wasn't wearing that ugly Bridesmaid Disaster. Isabella came over and stood next to me.

"Nice dress," she said. "I guess you're pretty happy the bridesmaids' dresses got stolen."

And then it hit me! Isabella had stolen the dresses. She was so touched that I passed on tacos with Hudson, that she did this for me.

"You shouldn't have done that, Isabella," I said. "I really appreciate it, but you shouldn't have stolen the dresses."

"I didn't steal them," she said. "I loved that dress. I wouldn't have done that for you."

And then Angeline walked up, and she said, "Nice dress, Jamie."

Suddenly I **REALLY** realized what had happened. Angeline had stolen the dresses for me. It makes sense. Angeline was so glad that I told the truth about the earrings that she did this for me in return.

"Angeline. You shouldn't have stolen the dresses for me. It was a nice gesture, but you shouldn't have done it."

For a second I felt a little regret that I wasn't related to her.

Awww. it was so nice of her to STEAL for me.

I might even visit her in JAIL.

Angeline laughed. "You're right Jamie, it **WOULD** have been a nice gesture, but I didn't do it. I loved that dress. I looked like a million bucks in it, and Isabella looked like a thousand bucks. I figured you stole them."

And then I was glad **AGAIN** that I'm not related to her.

How **DARE** Angeline think I might be A **CROOK!**

"Also," she added, "I don't know how I feel about being related to a thief."

"We're not related," I informed her. "We're not cousins."

"Of course we're not cousins," she said. "We're going to be *grandmas* together."

That's when Isabella just lost it. She started jumping up and down and screaming and begging me, "Can I have one, Jamie? Can I please please have one?"

I must have looked pretty confused because Angeline felt like she had to explain.

"Oh, c'mon, Jamie. Don't play dumb. You're the one that's been stuffing Stinker under our fence. I've seen you do it."

SHOVE

"It wasn't Jamie," Isabella admitted — although it sounded a lot more like bragging than admitting.

"I knew that Stinker and Stickybuns were in love that first night they met at Jamie's house," Isabella said. "They wanted to be together. And when two people are in love, they should be together. Even if one of those people is a dog. And so is the other one."

Can you believe how sweet Isabella is, giving so generously of her time so that Stinker and Stickybuns could spend time together? And that explains why Stinker kept coming back from the walks all scratched up. Isabella had been stuffing him under Angeline's fence.

"Are they going to have puppies?" Isabella asked, and I think that she very nearly squealed, which made it the first time I had ever heard her do anything like that.

"When will the puppies be here? Can I please have one? Please please please?"

Angeline grinned. "The vet says that Stickybuns is going to have puppies in three or four weeks. And sure, you can have one!"

Puppies. Stinker is going to be a dad. And Stickybuns is going to be a mom. That makes Angeline and me grandmas — *together.*

"What in the world did Stickybuns ever see in Stinker?" I said. He's my dog and everything. I know that I love him, but seriously: EW.

Isabella said, "He did poop some nice bling. You know *that* gots to impress the ladies."

She's right. But I'm not sure what's harder to accept: That now I really *am* related to Angeline (In-Laws by Dog) or the fact that there are a few burglars running around in those bridesmaids' dresses right now.

At least now I know what Isabella was hinting at with the spiders in my burrito and the snakes in my yard. She was hinting about the puppies.

At the end of the evening, I kissed Aunt Carol, congratulated her, and thanked her for everything. Then I went to say good-bye to Uncle Assistant Principal Devon. I caught up to him in the hall. I congratulated him and wished him a fun honeymoon.

"Bit of luck the dresses got stolen, huh?" he said, and he smiled this big dumb smile that I had not seen him smile in a month. It revealed more than just a mouthful of nice teeth.

"YOU stole them?" I asked him.

"I didn't say that," he said. "But I knew you hated that dress. I hated it, too. Your Aunt Carol and I had a huge argument about it. That's why she was crying a little that day."

"So you made the dresses disappear? For me?" I asked, even though I was totally sure of the answer.

HE DID IT.

All he said was that we'd talk about it when they got back from their honeymoon. He said he thought that the truth was still the truth even if it's a couple days late.

I told him that was the dumbest thing I'd ever heard.

I know what the truth is. The truth is that he's not a rat. The truth is he's my Uncle Dan.

## CAUTION

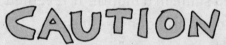

SOME TRUTH CAN'T WAIT A COUPLE DAYS:

LAST WEDNESDAY I LOST MY RABID MONKEY BY THE PRESCHOOL.

I ACCIDENTALLY BAKED A COUPLE WORMS INTO YOUR BIRTHDAY CAKE A YEAR AGO.

THANKS FOR ELECTING ME. I LIED ABOUT EVERYTHING.

# Sunday 28

Dear Dumb Diary,

    It's Sunday. Homework day, again. Isabella is coming over because she has no idea what to do with her diorama, since that whole "Baron Von Leash" thing was a load of garbage. (Note the flies around that.)

    But I think I know what my Discovery Diorama is going to be about.

    It's about what I've discovered about dumbness:

1.    It's pure dumbness to give up a Taco Rendezvous, and it's dumb to take the blame for something you didn't do.

2.    It's dumbness to think that you can invent a car or a plane or a microscope.

149

3. It's dumbness that makes dogs and people fall in love. Whether you're going to be crammed into a wedding dress or through a hole in a fence, love is a **LOT** of work.
4. It's dumbness that makes people collect things, give away puppies, decorate gyms, give gifts, love their stinky dogs, and dance like nobody is watching.
5. And it's dumbness that makes a person keep a diary.

But sometimes the very best things that people do are done out of dumbness. So the smartest thing to do is to never underestimate your dumbness.

Thanks for listening, Dumb Diary.

*Jamie Kelly*